IRRITATING IRVING
by TONY GARTH

Irving was usually a quiet and well-behaved little boy.

Unless, that is, he was bored.

When Irving had nothing to do, he became the most irritating boy in the world.

One sleepy Sunday afternoon, Irving was bored. He couldn't think of a single thing to do.

His Mum was cleaning the kitchen floor.

"Mum," said Irving. "I haven't got anything to do."

"Nonsense," said his Mum. "Why don't you go and play football in the garden?"

"Oh, all right," said Irving, and went outside to find his football.

Irving found his football and started to bounce it against the back door. Much to his Mum's annoyance.

Thump! thump! thump! Went the football against the back door.

Thump! thump! thump! Until his Mum couldn't stand it any longer. She opened the door and told Irving to stop. The muddy football flew into the kitchen and bounced mud all over her nice, clean floor.

"Oh, Irving!" she said. "Now look what you've done. Go and play in your room instead."

"Oh, all right," said Irving, and went upstairs.

"I know," thought Irving. "I'll practise my drumming."

He'd completely forgotten his Grandma who was having a nap in the room next door. She nearly jumped out of her skin when Irving started playing.

"For goodness sake, Irving," she said, shouting to make herself heard. "Can't you find anything quieter to do? Go and see what your Dad's doing?"

"Oh, all right," said Irving and went to find his Dad.

Irving's Dad was busy doing paperwork in his study.

"Just sit quietly and read your comic," he told Irving. "I need to concentrate on these numbers."

Irving sat down and began to read. He rustled his comic.

"Shhhh!" said his Dad.

Irving started to giggle at the antics of his favourite characters.

"Shhhh!" said his Dad.

The rustling and giggling went on and on until Irving's Dad couldn't stand it any longer.

"Why don't you go and see what Grandad is doing?" he said.

Grandad was building a model sailing ship. It was made entirely from matchsticks. He'd been working on it for months.

"Hello, Grandad," said Irving. "I'm looking for something to do."

"Don't come any closer," his Grandad said. "It's at a very tricky stage."

Irving's Grandad gave him a balloon to play with.

"Balloons are nice and quiet," he thought.

Irving blew up the balloon, stretched the end and let the air out with a loud screeching noise. It set his Grandad's teeth on edge.

"Aaagh! Stop!" he groaned.

Then Irving blew up the balloon again. This time he let it go.

The balloon flew around the room and narrowly missed the model ship.

"Irving!" said his Grandad. "Be careful!"

Irving blew up the balloon again. But this time he blew too hard and the balloon burst with a loud bang.

Irving's Grandad jumped with fright and... accidentally smashed the ship into a million pieces.

"I'll go and play somewhere else," said Irving.

He went to play on his computer but the noise irritated his big sister.

He played his favourite record but it irritated the dog.

Eventually his Mum decided to take him to the cinema and get him out from under everyone's feet.

It wasn't a good idea. The film was long and boring. Irving began to fidget. He sniffed loudly, rustled his bag of sweets and kicked the seat in front. He irritated everyone so much he and his Mum were asked to leave.

Eventually, it was time for bed. To everyone's relief. Soon, Irving was tucked up in bed and sleeping peacefully.

"What a day," sighed the whole family. "Still, at least he can't irritate anyone till morning."

Just then Irving began to snore...a very irritating snore.

Look out for the next twelve Little Monsters!

FRIENDLY FRANCO

CLUMSY CLARISSA

BOISTEROUS BILLY

SICKLY SIMON

SERIOUS SADIE

GROWN-UP GABBY

PERFECT PRUDENCE

RUDE ROGER

DANGEROUS DAVE

CURIOUS CALVIN

DIRTY DERMOT

TANTRUM TABITHA